The
Chosen
One

The Chosen One

Charles Blake Johnson

American Trail Books
Townsend

American Trail Books, Inc.
P.O. Box 400
Townsend, Tennessee 37882

ISBN 1-884505-01-5

Manufactured in the United States of America

First Edition

For Paul and Evelyn Johnson
and
In Memory of
Steve Yoder
(1948-1994)

"Blessed are the meek:
for they shall inherit the earth."
Matthew 5: 5

One

The young boy fought his way through the forest. Blackberry bushes tore at his arms, leaving bloody rips in his skin. Rocks tripped his feet, sending him tumbling to the ground. Still he moved onward, moving west alongside the river.

It began to rain. In the darkness he lost the trail. Tree limbs swung across in front of him, slapping his face hard. But he kept going, always hearing the flowing water just to the north.

He remembered his mother lying in bed dying of the white man's disease, the sickness of breath. Some called it smallpox. It had already killed many of the Real People who lived in Chilhowee Town, where he was born. He stood close to his mother as she struggled to breathe. When he touched her face, the dark skin burned hot. Even her breath came out hot when she spoke.

1

"Go to the Beloved Woman," she said. "There is no one left to care for you here now. Our people are dying in war, being killed by disease. In this place there is hardly a man left who can hunt. I do not want to leave you, son, but I must. Remember, find the Beloved Woman. She will care for you."

After she died that night, he sat outside watching the stars, wishing he could fly away like the owl or hawk. As the days passed, he grew more and more hungry, living on scraps of food. Then he took his small bow and hunted, sometimes killing a rabbit or small animal to eat.

He had always been different. His father was a white trader who lived among the Real People several years and then disappeared while on a trip to faraway Charles Town. From his earliest years, he was small and quiet and not good at games. The other boys laughed at him and called him Frog for reasons he never understood. Finally, that is how he came to think of himself.

In the old days, the Real People would have cared for a child of their own who had no home. Relatives would have rushed to help, to open their hearts. Now, with death and fear and change everywhere in Chilhowee Town, homeless children had to take care of themselves.

He left one night. No one saw him go. After he was gone, it was as though he never existed.

Going along the river, carrying his bow and a quiver of small arrows made with his own hands, he thought only of his mother's words and the Beloved Woman. Somehow, he must reach her. Somewhere, she waited for him.

He knew the Beloved Woman was the greatest woman of the Real People. This much he had heard many times, listening to the Chilhowee Town women talk. The Beloved Woman was the equal of any man of the Real People. She sat at the Council, always speaking for peace even when so many of the men wanted war.

To him, the Beloved Woman seemed the strongest, most beautiful woman who ever lived, even though he had never seen her. Surely she must possess magical powers. Maybe she could even fly! Yes, fly high above the world and away from all its troubles.

He ran west, toward the sacred town of Chota, where the Beloved Woman lived alongside the very river which guided him. At night he slept among the rocks and trees, listening to the sounds of the animals moving nearby. During the day, however, he could find no rabbits to shoot, no birds or squirrels waiting for his arrows, nothing to stop his hunger. So he kept going, stumbling through the woods until he was finally lost and starving. He put his head down on the ground and lay there looking up into the empty black sky. He could see no stars, no moon.

Maybe I will not wake, he thought. Maybe it is best that way.

When he felt the big hand on his face, he thought it might belong to a spirit. He opened his eyes and saw a fierce-looking man with smallpox scars covering his face. His earlobes had been stretched halfway to his shoulders and his head was plucked bald except for a scalplock that stood almost straight up.

"And what are you doing out here in the forest?" the man asked.

He could not answer.

"Who are you?" the man asked.

Again, he was silent.

"You won't say what clan you are born to, either," the man said.

By then more men gathered around the boy. They watched him as they might a captive deer.

"A lost one," the first man said. "And he won't talk."

"Starved, too, by the look of him," another man said.

"One more great warrior to be," said another one. "Starved and silent."

The men sat around him and fed him some dried meat. "Eat just a little," one said. "Warriors need their strength."

After he finished eating, the first man pulled him to his feet. "Come on and walk," he said. "You don't expect me to carry you to Chota?"

He felt stronger and walked fast to keep up with the men. They stopped now and then for water or to eat something, but he did not want to slow them down. Once, when they rested, the first man said, "My name is Five Killer. Now, who are you?"

But he did not feel like talking. If he talked, he would have to tell his story, and he wanted to save it for the Beloved Woman.

They came into Chota at last, going past the big Council House where the Beloved Woman sat with the important men of the Real People. They went by the chungke field, where a few men were playing the game, gambling on who could throw his pole nearest the stopping place of the rolling stone.

The men split up then going to their homes. Five Killer took him on, toward a large fine house built of logs.

A tall beautiful woman worked outside, stripping roots of their bark and then dropping them in a pot of boiling water hung over a fire. Five Killer hugged her, then said, "Mother, we found this lost boy half-dead in the woods today. He won't even tell us his name. I am not sure he can talk."

She dropped to her knees, looking into the boy's dark eyes. "He has had a bad time of it, that's easy to see," she said.

Her hand was warm when she picked up his. When she held him close to her body he felt as though she could have been his mother. She was older than his mother, and taller, but there was something very comforting about the way she touched him. She made him feel good.

"My name is Nanye'hi," she said.

He knew then that this woman, Five Killer's mother, was indeed the mother of them all. "The Beloved Woman!" he said. "I have come a long way to find you."

"He talks for you," Five Killer said. "For me he said not a word."

"And what brings you on this journey?" she asked the boy.

"My mother is dead. The white man's sickness killed her. She said to come to you, that you would care for me."

"Who is your father?"

"I don't know. A white man. He is gone."

"Did you know that my own father was a white man?" Nanye'hi asked.

"No!"

"As white as they come. All the way from England."

"Then you are like me?"

"Yes. It is of no matter who your parents may be. All that matters is who you are. And who are you?"

He looked at the ground. "They call me Frog," he said.

"Frog? Frog is no name for a boy," she said.

"It is all I have."

"No, it is not all you have. Today I give you a new name. You come to me from out of the woods on a special mission. You will do great things and be a great man. So I give you a new name to fit your spirit. You are now named Suyeta, The Chosen One."

"The Chosen One?"

"Yes. Do you not like it?"

"I am not worthy of such a name."

"You are worthy if you wish to be worthy," she said. "Do you?"

"Oh, yes," he said.

"Then from this day forward, you are The Chosen One."

He stood as tall as he could stretch then, putting his arms around the Beloved Woman, holding her tight. He would always remember his mother. He would always remember the horrors of Chilhowee Town. But now he was The Chosen One. Yes. It felt good on his tongue.

Two

The boy waited for magic. After all he had heard about the Beloved Woman, he expected her to do something wonderful and magical.

Instead, she put a hand on his shoulder. "You are hungry," she said.

She gave him a bowl of hominy. He sat on the ground beside her, eating noisily.

"Eat all you can," she said. "A hungry boy cannot think properly."

On her hearthstone, Nanye'hi shaped a loaf of corn bread, then covered it with a dish. She placed wood around the hearthstone and used an ember to fire it, so the flames burned hot around the bread.

"Now, while that bakes, we may talk," she said. "First, you say your mother said to come to me, but do you know why?"

"Because you are the Beloved Woman," he said with wonder.

"And that makes me like a mother to you?"

"Yes," he said. "A mother to us all."

"Do you know how I came to be the Beloved Woman?" she asked. He just shook his head and sat eating hominy, watching her.

"We were at a place called Taliwa. There was a great battle with our old enemies, the Creeks. I was young then, very young, and married to a young man called Kingfisher who was a very great warrior. But in this fight something very bad happened and King-fisher was killed," she said. She brought the long slen-der fingers of her hands to her face and stroked the skin, remembering the pain of the day long ago.

"I wanted to cry. I wanted to give up my own life and depart with him. But something took hold of me. Something from outside directed my actions. I picked up Kingfisher's weapons and began to fight. I shot and killed a man. I used the bow to kill more. Nothing could harm me then. The Creeks began to run and I chased them away. After the fight was done, the men called me the Beloved Woman. Back at Chota there was a big ceremony and I took on the duties of the Beloved Woman. They put the swan dress on my back, the swan fans in my hands. I learned how to make the black drink of war for the men. I took my place on the council, and I did my best for my people."

She pushed the burning wood closer around the hearthstone, then picked up one small glowing twig and blew on it, making the ember smoke and flame brighter. "The thing is, I am the Beloved Woman because the Real People say so. I will always be the Beloved Woman. But I am still the frightened young woman who went to battle that day with Kingfisher. The world around me changed but I did not change. I am still what I was. Do you understand?"

"I see it," the boy said. He was small and young and hungry, but he knew this was something to remember, these words from the Beloved Woman.

"Now you come to me, an orphan," she said. "You are alone in the world, and already you know much sadness. But I give you a new life. Life is more than what you put in your belly. It is more than anything you can touch or see. With this new life, I give you a new name, The Chosen One. But you will always be this hungry boy. You will always be the child who comes to me from the forest. Do you know this?"

"Yes," he said.

"So you and I, we are much alike. I am glad you found me, Chosen One."

When the bread was ready, she took it from the fire and served it to him hot. Five Killer came over then and sat beside him, eating.

"My son has a wife, but he prefers his mother's cooking," Nanye'hi said.

They ate in silence, sitting in the still afternoon listening to the sounds of the village, the children playing, the men yelling at chungke, the dogs barking. The Chosen One thought it was good to be among people again, to be among the living.

When they finished the bread, Nanye'hi stood and took his hand. "We will walk," she said, and they went through Chota, looking at the plots of corn and beans scattered between houses, talking quietly with other women, and then taking the trail out of the village. They paused along the river's bank at a spot Nanye'hi said was the grave of Oconostota, the Great Warrior of the Real People. Then they walked toward the old town of Tanasi, now empty and silent.

He watched as she bent and picked up a small stone, placing it on a pile of other stones by the pathway. "When I pass this spot, I always put another stone on the pile. It is to remember a good man killed by the enemy a long way from home, so far that the other men could not bring his body home. This is what we have to remember him by," she said. "I am a woman of peace but I honor my people. Without honor we have nothing."

The Chosen One watched her walk on down the path. He looked again at the pile of stones which grew day by day as the Beloved Woman passed this way, and he hoped someday someone might so honor him.

Three

From out of the dark forest one day another child came to Chota. It was a girl, smaller than The Chosen One, and even dirtier and hungrier than he had been when Five Killer found him.

One of the men brought her to the Beloved Woman's cooking fire. When Nanye'hi reached out a hand to touch her, she twisted away and ran to the riverbank, crawling in among a big tree root. Nanye'hi and Five Killer watched her go.

"Let her run," Five Killer said. "She will come back when she is hungry enough."

"She came to me," Nanye'hi said. "Now I must go to her."

Nanye'hi stirred the hominy in the pot, singing a bit to herself, then walked out the open door toward the river. She turned to The Chosen One.

"Will you help another in need?" she asked, offering him her hand.

He followed.

Though the Beloved Woman was no longer young, she walked quickly through Chota, her steps strong and sure. Looking up at her, The Chosen One thought she was still very beautiful, tall and straight and slender. He struggled to keep up as she made her way to the river called Tanasi.

"If a man or woman will not bend to help a child, then they may as well not live," she said. "If we do not live for our children, why should we live at all? What else do we have that matters to our hearts?"

They searched along the riverbank until they found her hiding among the tree roots. Nanye'hi stepped carefully toward the water, reaching down to touch the girl. But the girl fought back, pushing the Beloved Woman.

Nanye'hi laughed then. "You are a strong one, child, and full of fear. Never fight those who would help you," she said, bending low to look at the girl.

"Now, aren't you hungry? Wouldn't a nice pot of hominy taste good? We could eat a little and talk a little and learn something about each other."

The girl looked at her, then rose from the tree roots and held out her hand. "I am afraid," she said.

"Where is your mother?" Nanye'hi asked.

"I do not know," the girl said.

"And your father?"

"I do not have a father," the girl said.

"What is your clan?"

"Clan?" the girl asked.

"Where do you come from?"

"I cannot remember. It looked like this. There was a big water, a lot of people. I do not know its name. One day my mother was not there any more, so I left, and now I am here."

"You came to the right place," Nanye'hi told her. "You will be safe here."

"What is your name?" the girl asked.

"She is the Beloved Woman," The Chosen One said, amazed that any of the People would not know Nanye'hi.

"Wait," Nanye'hi said to him, then turned back to the girl. "My name is Nanye'hi. I was a little girl one time, too."

"You were?" the girl said.

"Yes. Just like you."

"Like me?"

The girl took Nanye'hi's hand and stepped up onto the riverbank. They stood there together, looking at the water and the birds skimming low near the surface.

"Yes. I was afraid, too. But I had a mother to take care of me. Would you like me to take care of you?"

The girl looked up and smiled for the first time. "Yes," was all she said.

"Come along then," Nanye'hi told her. "We have hominy in the pot."

They walked back through Chota to Nanye'hi's home. "This young fellow who thinks he knows everything is called The Chosen One," she said.

"That's a strange name," the girl said.

"A strange name for a strange boy. He came to me like you did, out of the forest one night and all alone. He can be your brother."

"I don't need a brother," the girl said.

"We all need a brother," Nanye'hi told her. "Someone to bring in a little fresh meat now and then. Even I needed a brother."

The Chosen One stepped up beside them, trying to make himself a little taller. Now he had someone to protect.

He felt proud. Everyone needs a brother, and now he was one.

Four

The girl settled into Nanye'hi's log home, working in the fields tending to the corn and vegetables, helping to scrape the hearth clean for baking bread. With time and food, she filled out and began and run and play with the other children.

Nanye'hi named her Astai'yi, "Strong Girl". Like The Chosen One, she didn't remember her real name. It didn't matter because now she started a new life.

"You survived when others would have died," Nanye'hi told her at her naming ceremony. "You have a mighty will. Already you are a wise one. You know that nothing good comes easy. You know the Real People must struggle to become great."

Nanye'hi looked over the river at the forest on the distant bank. To The Chosen One, her eyes seemed to see something far away that no one else saw. She stood a long time, then turned back to them.

"The two of you have no family, but now you have each other," she said. "You have no parents, so you belong to all the Real People. You must take what you learn and use it for the benefit of all. You came into the world at a hard time. Your lives will not be easy. Prepare yourselves for great things. That is the only way."

So Strong Girl and The Chosen One lived together, watching the Beloved Woman from day to day. Others began to come to Chota, asking her for help. There were many orphans, their mothers and fathers killed by war or disease. There were many widows, also, women whose husbands died in the fighting. They came to Chota, wondering if the Beloved Woman could do anything for them.

Nanye'hi gave them food to eat and a place to sleep. They worked alongside her in the fields, helped feed her cattle, watched over the younger children, and learned her lessons.

In the warm soft light at the end of one day, Nanye'hi took The Chosen One for a walk along the edge of Chota. He loved to be alone with her, when she could talk just to him.

"When I was a young girl about your age the old men told me the story of the magic lake," she said. "Do you know about it?"

"No," he said, standing close beside her.

"Up in the mountains, in the Land of Blue Smoke, is the lake called Ataga'hi," she said. "We know it is there but none of the Real People have ever seen it. Only the animals know exactly how to find it.

"But there was a man who wanted to find it. He first purified himself by fasting and prayer. He went to the place where the lake might have been. It was flat and dry and empty and nothing was there, not an animal, not a fish or a bird.

"All night long he stayed up, praying and fasting. Then at daybreak, the lake was there. The water was deep and bright, and it poured from the hills and cliffs of the mountains. There were many fish living in the water, and turtles and frogs and all sorts of wondrous things. Overhead there were many birds, ducks and pigeons. All around him were the tracks of animals, of deer and bear and skunks and beaver.

"As he sat there on the shore of the lake, a great bear came from the forest and told him its secrets. This was the medicine lake of all the animals, the bear said. If a hunter wounded a bear, the bear made its way here and bathed in the waters of the lake and the lake healed it. If a deer hurt itself, the water would heal it.

"Because the man had purified himself and became holy and wanted to know the secret, the bear told him about the lake. But no one else must know, the bear said, because the lake was for the animals only. It was where the animals came to escape from the hunters, so the lake must remain invisible to people," Nanye'hi said, stopping by the river.

"The man thought it would be wonderful, though, if people could share the lake's healing powers. He tried to argue with the bear, explaining that people would honor the sacredness of the lake and not harm the animals there. But the bear would not listen to what the man said. Go home, the bear told him. Go home and forget this place.

"So the man went home and told his story. Then he and some others went back to that spot in the mountains. They fasted and prayed but they never saw the lake. The great bear never spoke to them. Since that time the lake has been invisible to us. We know it is there, but we cannot see it."

"Can I go there?" The Chosen One asked.

"No, you cannot go there, but the lake, I think, is somehow inside you. You can give yourself the power to heal your people. They need a magic lake, they need something powerful and sacred to make them whole again. We have fought wars and we lost. We have gotten diseases and they killed many of us. Our land is being taken from us by the unakas, the whites. We are torn apart by our own disagreements. We need healing. Maybe you are the one. Maybe you can reach deep down inside yourself and find the healing lake for our people."

"Me? I am just a boy," he said.

"And I am an old woman. We are a fine pair, the two of us. What can we do? What can anybody do? We can do our best, that is what we can do. When we do our best, then maybe good things can happen. Tonight, you start."

"Tonight?" he asked. "What happens tonight?"

"Tonight you go with the old men. Tonight you begin to learn about your people and maybe about yourself. You will be the fire keeper."

"What do I do?" he asked.

"You will know when the time comes. I have spoken."

He watched as she turned and walked home, leaving him by the river. Looking up, he saw a hawk high above, circling in the air currents, searching for something.

Five

The Chosen One went that night to the sweat lodge, the asi, where the older men were gathering. Nanye'hi had told him how to build the fire and keep it going while the men talked. But she refused to go there herself.

"Some things are for the men only, just as some are for the women," she told him before sending him on his way.

Looking at the men as they stood outside the low log building, he grew afraid. He had never been around the men much. His life revolved around Nanye'hi, the Beloved Woman. She had no men living with her, and needed none.

The men looked fierce. Some were scarred from battle, others scarred from smallpox. They talked very little, waiting to begin the ceremony. He saw

Five Killer standing there with a friend, saying nothing. But Five Killer saw him and smiled, so he felt a little better.

He went inside, arranging the wood for the fire as Nanye'hi had told him. As the sun went down, the men settled into their places around the fire, stooping under the low roof. No one spoke until a very old man passed his hand over the fire. He leaned forward and said, "We are the Ani-Yun Wiya, the Real People, and we have the knowledge of life. The animals speak to us. The sun and the moon give us their gifts. The trees and rocks, the rivers and the very soil of the earth are part of us."

The men nodded in agreement. This was a story they had heard many times. It was new for The Chosen One, though. He listened. The story was a wonder, he thought, a great wonder. It was his story. He was part of it and it was part of him.

The old man who talked was the myth-keeper. He knew the story of the Real People all the way back to the beginning of time. His white hair fell far down his back. His fingers were gnarled and bent, his face lined with wrinkles. But his eyes were very wise, and The Chosen One understood that the old man knew everything that was important to the Real People. What he knew could fill the world.

"When I was a boy, the old men told me the secret of fire," the old man said. "The world was cold because there was no fire when people came here. Then the Thunders caused fire to live in a tree on an island in the river. The animals saw the smoke but could not use the fire because it was on the island. First the raven tried to fly after it and bring some back to shore. But it burned his feathers, so he failed.

"Then the Screech-Owl went after it but the smoke hurt his eyes. The Hoot-Owl and the Horned Owl went after it but they did no better. So the birds gave up.

"The black snake swam to the island and got to the tree. But the ashes of the fire burned him so he is still black today.

"Now the animals were very afraid. The bravest animals could not bring back the fire and they needed it very badly because the world was so cold. No one wanted to go after it, though.

"After a while, the water spider decided to try to get it. So she ran on top of the water to the island. She spun a web and made it into a bowl, which she carried to the tree. Then she very quickly put a tiny spark of the fire into the bowl and fast like the wind carried it back across the water to the other animals.

"They used it to start their own fire, and it kept them warm through the cold winter. Since that day we have had the blessing of fire. All because of the tiny water spider, who could do what the bravest could not."

The Chosen One looked into the fire he tended. It appeared new, clean and fresh, a part of the story of the Real People. He put another pine knot into it, watching it blaze higher.

The old man bent even lower, looking closely at The Chosen One, then at the others around the circle. "When I was young, the old men told me about Kana'ti, the hunter," he said.

"The hunter had two sons. One was born from his wife, Selu, in the way of all children. The other was born in the river, from the blood where the hunter washed his meat. The two sons played together at the river bank but the one born in the river, the Wild Boy, never stayed with them. They could not entice him inside. Then one day, the two boys wrestled and the hunter came and caught the Wild Boy and took him home with him.

"So he lived with the family. He was full of tricks, though, and got into all sorts of trouble. One day the Wild Boy took his brother and they followed the hunter when he went to the woods. The hunter went into a swamp and began making arrowshafts from the reeds that grew there. The Wild Boy used his powers and changed into some bird's down, like comes from a baby bird, and floated over the swamp until he came to the hunter. Then he settled down onto the hunter's shoulder and the hunter never even knew it. Wild Boy watched but he didn't know what the hunter was doing as he made his arrows.

"When the wind blew the bird's down away and into the woods, Wild Boy became human again. He and the other boy followed the hunter into the woods and up the mountainside. They hid behind a tree and watched as he lifted a big rock. From the hole where the rock had been, a big buck deer ran out. The hunter shot it and took it home.

"The boys then thought they knew the secret of the hunter and how he kept them supplied with meat. All he has to do is let a deer out of the hole and then kill it anytime the family needs meat, they decided.

"So the boys waited some time, then went to the swamp and cut reeds to make their arrows. They went up the mountain and lifted the rock. A deer ran out. When they were about to shoot it, another deer ran out, and then another and another and another. All the deer escaped from the hole and ran into the forest. After them came the raccoons and rabbits, the squirrels and skunks. All the four-footed animals. Then the birds came, the turkey and the pigeons, all the game birds. They flew out with such a noise that the hunter sitting at home heard the sound like thunder and knew right away the boys were doing something wrong. So he ran up the mountainside and was very mad when he found the boys by the rock, with the hole open and the animals escaped.

"The hunter jumped into the hole and from jars in the corners released the fleas, the lice, the ticks, the gnats, and the bedbugs. These stung and bit the boys until the boys were exhausted. At last the hunter made the bugs go away, and told the boys to go home.

"Now things would be different, he told them. Once, whenever they were hungry, all he to do was come to this place and release an animal or turkey and shoot it. Then they could eat. Now they would all have to hunt in the forest for anything they ate.

Never again would it be easy to feed a family. Now they would have to work for it, and sometimes come home without anything at all.

"So the boys went home and the hunter went to the forest to try to find something to eat. And that is why we must now hunt for a living."

The old man continued telling stories, about Selu and how the Real People came to have corn, about when the boys fought the wolves and burned nearly all of them up in a fire, about the time the boys escaped from the cannibals.

It was magical to hear these stories of the Real People, The Chosen One thought. He tended the fire, listening all night. When the old man grew tired and quit talking, another man took up the story-telling, and then another. Even Five Killer told some tales.

Then at daybreak the story-telling stopped. The men rose from around the fire and went outside, stretching their bodies because they had been cramped inside the small space all night. They all walked to the river and stood there quietly.

The old man who started the story telling, touched The Chosen One. "Remove your shirt," he said.

The Chosen One stared at him, open-mouthed.

"Now," the old man said.

So he took the shirt off and stood there bare-chested. The old man then reached into a leather bag and took out a bone-tooth comb. He turned The Chosen One around and scratched his back with the comb. The boy wanted to cry out because it hurt to be scratched like that, but he said nothing. Something about the stories he had heard that night made him keep silent.

When the old man was through scratching his back with the comb, he took The Chosen One and they waded into the water until it was almost to the boy's chin. The water was cold and he was shaking with fear and chill. But the other men followed into the water and still The Chosen One kept quiet.

"Face the sun," the old man told him.

He looked toward the east, where the sun was rising. The sky was red and orange where the ball of fire rose somewhere beyond the Land of Blue Smoke.

The old man put a hand on the boy's head and pushed it under water. The Chosen One came up, sputtering and shaking. But the old man began to pray for him, praying that he might become a true member of the Real People, one worthy of the old stories.

He dunked the boy under the water again. And when he came up, again the old man prayed. Seven times altogether the boy's head was pushed into the water, and seven times the old man prayed.

By the time he was finished, the sun was up and light filled the sky. "The Beloved Woman has named you The Chosen One," the old man said at last. "That is a good name. May you live to fulfill it."

The men took him back to Nanye'hi's home then. He was wet and cold but somehow very happy. He had been given the knowledge of the Real People. He had a family, and his family was all the People, everywhere.

Six

One day Nanye'hi called The Chosen One and Strong Girl in to talk with her as she baked corn and bean bread. She had already used lye to soften the corn. Now she pounded the grains into meal and mixed it with cooked beans. As she talked, she made loaves of the dough, then wrapped them in corn husks. These went into the hot ashes of the fire.

Chota, she said, had always been a great town of the Real People. It was a peace town, a place of refuge, where people in trouble could come to work out their problems. It was the capital town of the Real People, and they met here in their councils to decide how the people should live.

For many years Chota had been this way. Yet even before Chota there had been another town very nearby called Tanasi. This town, which was abandoned by the people when they moved to Chota, gave its name to the river that flowed by their door. Now the Americans, who had won the great war for this country against the British, called this whole area Tanasi.

During that war, Nanye'hi said, the American army had moved down the river from the mountains, burning all the towns of the Real People, including Chota. Many people had died in the fighting. Nanye'hi herself had been arrested and held until they let her go to return here and help rebuild Chota.

But Chota was no longer the same, she said. The Americans were moving in all around Chota, crowding the people, even though their own treaty said they could not live here. Now the hunting was very poor. It was hard to live in the old way.

Some of the Real People insisted on fighting the Americans. They did this even though the years had proven that fighting did no good. Her own cousin, the famous Dragging Canoe, son of the even more famous Little Carpenter, had led a group of the Real People to a place near Lookout Mountain, a group of new towns on Chickamauga Creek. From there, they raided the American settlements, refusing to give up their old way of life.

"In the end, it will come to nothing," Nanye'hi said. "They will die and our world will keep on changing. We cannot stop it."

The real Chota would fly like a hawk to the sun and then be only a memory, she told them.

"Someday we will leave this place, though we carry it in our hearts forever," she said.

Strong Girl and The Chosen One had already been slipping away to play with the American children who lived nearby. There were not many children left in Chota, so it was natural that they would be curious about their new neighbors.

But more and more American families moved to the land near Chota. Some had trouble with the children from Chota, wanting to fight. One day The Chosen One and Strong Girl were directly across the river from Chota, playing games with the others.

Strong Girl ran into one of the American girls, not meaning to, and knocked her down. An American boy, a big tall boy, came and pushed Strong Girl to the ground, kicking her.

"Dirty Cherokee," he said. "You keep your dirty stinking hands off my sister."

Strong Girl looked up. She knew enough of the language the Americans spoke to understand what the boy said. "I did not mean to do it," she said.

"No, you never mean to do nothing, do you, you dirty Indians," he said. Then he kicked her.

He wore heavy black boots with big soles, and the kick hurt Strong Girl. She cried out, and then he kicked her again, and again.

Now The Chosen One had seen what was happening. He ran across the open ground by the river and, never stopping, jumped the American boy, pulling him away from Strong Girl. They rolled on the ground, then two more of the American boys piled on, hitting and kicking The Chosen One.

Strong Girl tried to pull them off him but they were too big and just shoved her away. She stood back, crying, watching them beat him.

Then the boy who started it all had the other two hold The Chosen One. "You dirty Indians can't get away with this," he said. "You can't go around acting like you're white people. You have to pay for this."

He pulled out a knife. It was not large, but the blade shone in the sunlight and looked very dangerous.

"No!" Strong Girl yelled.

"You're next," the boy said, looking at her. "You're next."

The knife swept at The Chosen One. Somehow he ducked to one side, though, and it slipped down until it cut his arm. Blood spurted out and seemed to scare the other boys. They let him go and he spun away from them until he was standing next to Strong Girl.

"You are here only because we let you live in this place," The Chosen One said to the American boys. "We could kill you any time we want."

The boys began to laugh then. The big one cleaned The Chosen One's blood from his knife blade with a handful of grass.

"We are people of peace and that is the only reason we have not already killed you," The Chosen One said. "You are the treaty breakers."

The boys continued laughing. He took Strong Girl's hand and pulled her away.

"Come on," he said. "Let's get away from these water-dogs."

They crossed the river and went home. Nanye'hi saw his arm and wrapped it with some cloth to make the bleeding stop. She looked very sad as he told her what had happened.

Finally, she stood up and looked out the open door of her home. "The time has come," she said. "Now we must leave Chota."

The Chosen One moved up beside her. "Don't move because of what happened to me. I won't go over on that side of the river any more," he said.

"It makes no difference," she said. "Chota is like an old man ready to die. Nothing we do for him will stop it."

Strong Girl began to cry. Nanye'hi turned to her.

"We have no time for that," she said. "We must get ready for our new lives."

Seven

They left with all they had packed into three wagons pulled by mules. The Chosen One helped three other boys drive Nanye'hi's cattle behind the wagons. They went south, to the Amovey District and the Ocoee River where Nanye'hi's brother, Long Fellow, lived.

At first they stayed with Long Fellow. Then, as more people came to see if the Beloved Woman could help them, Nanye'hi grew restless, wanting a place of her own where she could take care of them. She rented a farm and began growing crops.

George Washington, the American president, sent word to the Ani-Yun Wiya that he wanted them to survive by farming. So Nanye'hi planted cotton and peanuts, in addition to the corn she already knew how to grow. She kept chickens, and milked her cows.

When she had enough money from the crops, Nanye'hi bought an inn at the Womankiller Ford of the Ocoee River. There she let all the orphans and widows live who had come to depend on her. There was plenty of room. The hallways and porches filled with laughter as the children played.

But to The Chosen One, who was growing older now, the good times on the Ocoee seemed small compared to what he remembered at Chota on the Tanasi. And every day people came to see their Beloved Woman, thinking she could somehow save them. They were poor and starving, bringing nothing with them but taking much.

He tried to get Nanye'hi to put a stop to this flood of people. "There is no more room," he told her. "We cannot feed them all."

She shook her head. "Never," she said. "These are my people and my home is always open to them."

And so they lived there in peace, taking in all who asked. Nanye'hi's warlike cousin Dragging Canoe died, and even the Ani-Yun Wiya who lived and fought with him at the Chickamauga Towns wanted the fighting to end.

Some of the children in the house began to get sick, though. They became very hot with fever and could not sleep. One of the smaller children died, despite everything Nanye'hi and the other women could do.

Then Strong Girl got the fever. In her bed she spoke strange words and was afraid that wild animals were going to eat her. She could not sleep and did not know anyone that tried to help her.

Nanye'hi got The Chosen One and they went to the forest. She was looking here and there, searching for something.

"What are we looking for?" he asked.

"Snakeroot," she said.

"Maybe we should get an American doctor to give her medicine," he said.

"I can help her," she said. "I have the power to heal. So do you, only you do not yet know it. Some snakeroot will do it. So get to looking and forget about the American doctor."

They finally found some snakeroot. Back home, Nanye'hi ground it into a powder, then mixed it with water, brewing it into a tea. She forced Strong Girl to drink it. Then Nanye'hi bent low over her, touching her forehead with both hands, whispering something to the sick girl.

Before long Strong Girl began to get better. The fever cooled and she began to talk.

She reached out for The Chosen One's hand and pressed it to her cheek. "My brother," she said.

He let her hold his hand as long as she wanted, glad to see her living as a normal child again.

"My brother," she said again, and he liked the sound of it. He was her brother. The old men said so, as did Nanye'hi. Now he felt it deep inside.

In his time away from the fields he built a sweat lodge so the old men would have a place to come and share their stories. He loved to hear them say, "When I was a boy the old men said to me," and then begin their tales of the Thunderers, or the old days when the Shawano raided the Ani-Yun Wiya from the north and from the south the Creeks fought over hunting land boundaries, of The Ice Man, the sun and moon.

One night as he built the fire for the men, an old one took him aside. "Let a little one tend the fire," he said. "You know the stories. You sit with the men from now on."

So he became a man, a man among the other men in a hard time. But it felt good.

One day Nanye'hi told him a story of the Nunne'hi, the little people, the spirit people who lived under the mountains and even under the waters, and who had given Nanye'hi her name. He had heard of the Nunne'hi, of course, but this story was a new one.

"On the Hiwassee River a long time ago, the people heard the Nunne'hi calling, telling them of wars to come, of hunger and hatred and horror. The Nunne'hi said, 'Come live us. You will like it and will escape these bad things.'

"They said to go into the townhouse and fast for seven days, all the while being very quiet and prayerful. Since the Real People in that place were very afraid of these bad things to come, they decided to do it.

"So they had been in the townhouse for six days with no problem. On the seventh day they heard thunder roaring their way from the Land of Blue

Smoke. The ground began to shake and they were now very scared, so some of the women began to cry out.

"At that very moment, the Nunne'hi were there to carry away the townhouse. But when the women cried out, they dropped a corner of it and it formed a mound we can see to this day. Then they grouped together and picked up the townhouse again and carried it away to the mountains, to the top of a mountain, and set it down.

"We go there now and see a big rock. But the people of that town are there inside the mountain living with the Nunne'hi. They escaped from all this trouble because they believed. Now they will live forever in happiness.

"That is one reason we can never leave this land. If we do, we leave behind these people of ours, these kinsmen. They are a part of us," she said.

"Then why do they not help us in our time of need?" The Chosen One asked.

"Maybe they are trying and we cannot hear," she said.

"But my ears are open. My heart is open. Still I hear nothing from them," he said. "If the Nunne'hi would help them, why not us?"

"I think it is too late," she said. "I think the time for help is past."

He walked for a long time along the river that day, thinking about these things. Nanye'hi was growing old but she was still the Beloved Woman and the wisest person he had ever known. She had taken him in when he was a child wandering in the forest and then saved his life many times.

If the time for help was past, then why were the Real People still here? They could be strong. They could be a fierce and respected people as they had once been. If they needed help, then he would give them that help.

After all, was he not The Chosen One?

He sat very quietly as the day darkened. With night coming on, he watched a fox stalking a mouse in the rocks near the river. With a quick movement, the fox had the mouse in its jaws. For the mouse, life ended. But the fox lived on to hunt another day, to run and play and be a fox.

Is it not better to be the hunter than the hunted? he asked himself. He rose and walked back toward the inn. Nanye'hi would be wondering where he had gone. But these things were on his mind. If he was a man now, he must do those things a man did, taking care of his people.

As he walked back, the Milky Way popped out in the sky. It pointed the way home, a good sign.

Eight

With the hunting growing poorer every year, there was little to keep a young man like The Chosen One busy. Not so very long ago, he would have lived much of his life in the forests and on the trails. Now he stayed close to home most of the time, helping Nanye'hi and Strong Girl and the others in the fields.

This was woman's work. But with nothing else to do, hoeing the weeds from corn and cotton seemed a small thing. His hand grew used to the plow so the wooden handles seemed made to fit him. He even grew to enjoy the cows, feeding and handling them, working with the young calves.

But Nanye'hi understood that all this was not enough for him or the other young men on the Ocoee. So there beside the river they held a Green

Corn Dance as the Real People had for many, many years. Many of the young ones had never seen this festival. The older people, who came from far away, showed them what to do.

The Chosen One was most excited about the ball-play. This was a sport for the young men only. They divided into teams, the home-team of the Ocoee River men against all the rest. The players used ball-play sticks with webbing in a curve to catch a deer-skin ball and throw it over a goal post to score a point.

It was a hard thing to do, however. The players from the other team were allowed to tackle or hit or kick the men with the ball. There were no penalties, and no crying.

In the old days players were sometimes killed on the field by their opponents as they fought for the ball. Nothing like that happened on this day, but The Chosen One thought he might die several times. Once as he ran down the field, a huge player from the other team smashed into him, knocking him down and stealing away the ball. He rose from the ground to find blood streaming from his nose.

That made him angry, so he dashed after the big man and took the ball back, avoiding the fierce blows directed at his ribs. He ran down the field, swerving to avoid the other team's players. One swiped at his legs with a ball-play stick, knocking him down, but he still kept the ball and scrambled to his feet. He made his way toward the goal post and, narrowly missing a last charge from the big man who had bloodied his nose, threw the ball over it for a point.

On all sides the older men, women and children, along with a few white men, watched. At sundown the game ended with the score tied. He came off the field barely able to walk and stretched out under a big tulip poplar tree. Strong Girl came up then with another young woman, The Fawn, who lived with other members of her Bird Clan not far away up the river.

Strong Girl offered him water as The Fawn stood back and watched. "You were very quick," The Fawn said. "For one who has played so little, you are good at the ball-play. You run like the wolf."

"I am a wolf," The Chosen One said, and it was true. Nanye'hi was a member of the Wolf Clan, so through her he was a wolf, also. He looked up at The Fawn and rather than the girl he would have seen not long ago, he saw a young woman standing tall and beautiful next to the tree. With her long hair and fine features she looked much like he imagined Nanye'hi had looked many years ago.

Then The Fawn turned and walked away, back toward her family. He rose to his feet but Strong Girl put a hand on his arm, keeping him from following her.

"She will come back," Strong Girl said, laughing a little. "It is all she can do to stay away."

The festival lasted several days. At the end, Nanye'hi prepared the black drink, the same drink she used to prepare for men going to battle, and the young men drank it to purify themselves. Then they bathed in the river and came forth clean and fresh. On the final night there was one more dance.

The Chosen One did his part, dancing with the other men, then watched as The Fawn danced with the women. She moved lightly, smoothly. Her eyes flashed when she looked at him across the fire.

He wanted to talk with her but waited until seven days after the festival ended before going to her family's log house down the river from Nanye'hi's. After that, he went to see her as often as he could, and they talked for many hours. He told her about his dreams for helping the Real People, and she understood what he felt. She felt the same way, she said.

One day he went out hunting. He did it the old way, with bow and arrows. Up a creek that fed into the Ocoee he spent most of the day watching an animal trail, hoping to find game. Near dusk a buck deer came down to water.

The Chosen One calmly fitted an arrow in the bow and fired, making a clean kill. He carried the deer back home, cleaned the carcass, then took it to The Fawn's home. Using a strong rope, he hung it from a tree limb by the house, then left without saying a word to the young woman.

He went home and told Nanye'hi what he had done. "It is good for a man to have a wife," she said. "But these are hard times for our people. I see even harder times coming. You must be a strong man to have a family in these days."

In the morning, Nanye'hi went to The Fawn's home and talked with her mother and father. To The Chosen One, waiting at home, she seemed to be gone many hours.

Finally, she came home, and went directly to the field, working in the corn.

He went out to see her. "Well, what do they say?" he asked.

She bent to pick a striped worm off a leaf, grinding it in the dust beneath her foot. "What do they say? They say yes, of course. What do you expect them to say?" she said.

So The Chosen One and The Fawn became husband and wife. There was no big ceremony. On the appointed day she came to him dressed in a white deer skin decorated with many fancy things, with beads and porcupine quills and tassels and feathers. She gave him an ear of corn and promised to be a good housekeeper.

That was all it took. When all the people were gone he held her close as they stood on the porch of the inn, looking out over the river valley. Where they had been one, now there were two. He was truly a man.

Nine

As The Chosen One's life changed, so did the lives of the Real People. One spring day he and Five Killer left to see what had become of their old land.

Five Killer was old enough to have fought against the Creeks in the old days, to have even ridden against the Americans a time or two in the great war despite the Beloved Woman's wishes for peace. Riding on horseback, Five Killer told what it was like to have to kill in battle, and to fight next to men of his childhood who fell under enemy fire.

"It was a terrible time," Five Killer said.

"At least you did something for your people," The Chosen One said.

"What did I do?" Five Killer asked. "Fire a gun a few times? Yell and run like a madman? I do not know what it was all for."

They rode in silence then, making their way up the old trails to the place where Chota had been. Sitting on horseback on a hill overlooking the river valley, they saw white men working the fields Nanye'hi and the other women of the Ani-Yun Wiya tended for so many years. Most of the old houses were gone. The Americans lived in a few but the rest had been torn down.

All around the old town site the forests had been cut to make more fields. Cattle grazed in the places The Chosen One had played as a child. Fires burned piles of trees, leaving a smoky haze covering everything.

Five Killer turned his horse away. "I have seen enough," he said. They headed for Tellico Blockhouse, getting some supplies from the agent there, and rode up the Hiwassee River to the place where a Presbyterian preacher, Reverend Gideon Blackburn, ran a school to educate the children of the Ani-Yun Wiya.

They saw a small log building, with about 20 children outside it sitting in a circle. Reverend Blackburn and his wife sat in the center of the circle, turning to face the children as they slowly read from a book. As Five Killer and The Chosen One watched from the trees, the children picked up another book and began to sing. The Chosen One knew enough English to understand that the children were singing about the white man's god.

Though Five Killer and The Chosen One did not think children needed to know how to read or write or sing to live in the old way, they knew the old way was dying. Had they not just come from Chota? Nanye'hi herself had heard of Reverend Blackburn's school and approved of it.

"For our people to survive with the whites, we must understand those things that are important to the whites," she had said.

When they rode into the clearing, the singing stopped. Some of the children looked afraid. Reverend Blackburn stood and spoke to them. When he learned who Five Killer was, he insisted that they stay to eat a meal cooked by Mrs. Blackburn.

Reverend Blackburn grew very excited about his guests. After the meal, which was much like their meals back home on the Ocoee, Reverend Blackburn asked Five Killer to tell the children about Nanye'hi.

"A lot of these children know nearly nothing about the history of their own people," Reverend Blackburn said. "It should be part of their educaton to learn their culture and their heritage. I would be honored to have you tell your mother's story."

Five Killer waited a short while, then stood as he had seen the wise men of the Real People stand before a group, and said, "They call my mother the Beloved Woman. She is a very great person. I will tell you why."

The Chosen One listened as Five Killer spoke of this woman who was surely his own mother, too. But Five Killer knew the whole story. He told how she fought the Creeks after his father died in battle, winning the title of the Beloved Woman, and of how ever after she worked for peace, never again fighting in war. He told of the many times she spoke in treaty conferences, trying to get the Americans and the Real People to understand they must live together.

"Many times she set captives free," Five Killer said. "Many times she saved the Americans in their forts and settlements. She brought leadership to our people and made us realize that our way can not be the way of war."

The children sat, awed by this strong man who told such a wondrous story. One little girl stood up. "Is your mother holy?" she asked.

Five Killer paused before answering. The Real People did not believe in holy people in the manner of the Americans. In their own way, they believed all things were holy.

"Is the Beloved Woman holy? Yes, I think she is," he said. "She walks with the spirits."

As Five Killer and The Chosen One prepared to leave, Reverend Blackburn spoke quietly to them. "Give a message to the Beloved Woman for me," he said. "I know she has much power, sitting on the council of the Real People as she does. Tell her the Real People must change even more. Tell her they must have a government like the Americans. They must have laws and courts and government officials. That is the only way for them to survive."

Five Killer mounted his horse. "You may speak the truth," he said. "But it will be a sad day when we stop walking as free people and live as the Americans do."

They rode away, south past what was left of the Chickamauga towns, skirting onward alongside Lookout Mountain to Will's Town, where they stayed several days, then crossed the mountain to the place of the Ani-Yun Wiya the Americans now called Georgia. Here they saw large plantations with many slaves working in cotton fields. Some of these places were even owned by people who were mixed-bloods, part white and part Ani-Yun Wiya.

"It is not a good thing to own so much land," Five Killer said. "Land is not a thing that can be owned. Land belongs to all. How can we own the air we breath or the water we drink or the ground we walk upon? A man can own nothing but himself."

The Chosen One agreed. "It is not good to own other people, either," he said. The Real People had long owned slaves. They took war captives and made them work the fields, and sold them to the Americans in Charles Town. The Chosen One had always seen slaves, but never had he seen so many working in one place.

"Nothing here is good," Five Killer said.

They turned their horses northward, setting out for the Ocoee and home. Once there, The Chosen One found The Fawn waiting for him in the shade of their log home. She laughed as he held her close. He started to tell her what he had seen, but she put a finger to his lips, shushing him.

"I have something to tell first," she said.

"Tell it then," he said.

"I am expecting a child," she said.

For the moment he forgot what he saw on the trip, sitting on the ground by their doorway, letting the horse graze grass along the nearby river. He pulled her to his side and they lay there together. Overhead he saw a cloud, and in the cloud he saw the shape of a swan. It was a good sign, for the swan was the symbol of the Beloved Woman.

Ten

The Fawn gave birth to a girl. Because of The Chosen One's vision, and to honor Nanye'hi, the child was called Swan. She grew strong and Nanye'hi visited often, sitting with Swan and singing softly to her until she slept.

Strong Girl married a young Deer Clan man named Hawk. Soon, she also had a child, a boy called Black Fox. The Chosen One was pleased to see the young woman he called sister living a happy life. It seemed strange to see her now, though, with a child and a husband. Stranger still, people now called her Strong Woman. She was too old to be called a girl any more.

Working his farm, The Chosen One grew more troubled by what happened to his people. In Georgia, three leaders, the famous Doublehead, Tahlonteskee, and James Vann, a rich man whose plantation The Chosen One had seen on his trip with Five Killer, took money to sign a treaty giving away some of the Real People's land. It was a big piece of ground, one they had fought over many times against the Creeks. The Americans wanted it to clear the way for a road leading from Georgia to the young town of Nashville. Now that land was gone forever.

Around the Ocoee and the Hiwassee, the men of the Real People were angered by the treaty. A young man growing in the people's respect, Ridge, and another man tracked down Doublehead and killed him as he hid in the loft of Gideon Blackburn's school. This divided the Real People even more. It seemed possible they might actually fight among themselves.

Soon the new American president, Thomas Jefferson, told the people living around the old Chickamauga Towns that they could move west of the Mississippi River to a place called Dardanelle Rock and live there. To avoid a fight, more than a thousand left their native country, gone to a harsh land.

All this troubled The Chosen One very much. Nanyc'hi, too, was bothered by it.

"We must never leave this land," she said. "Without this land, what are we? We do not own this land but it owns us."

At the festivals of spring, summer and harvest, the men spoke of nothing else but the split among their people. Some blamed the mixed bloods who were becoming more powerful and ever richer on their farms and plantations.

On a day so hot even the young men wanted to do nothing but sit in the shade of the trees, word came to the festival that the Americans and the English were again at war. This caused much talk among the people.

The young men of their old enemies the Creeks were on the side of the English, and already raiding against the whites living along their border. Tecumseh, a leader of the Shawano, the Real People's old enemy to the north, traveled all the way to the Creek country to speak against the Americans. He wanted to throw off all whites, do away with all the things of the whites, and band all the tribes together to make a stand.

So the Real People called a medicine dance at Ustanali, in Georgia. The council gathered and met, with The Chosen One going along with Nanye'hi, as was now his custom. He spoke with Ridge, who already sat on the council even though he was still young.

At Ustanali, men from the Creeks came and asked for the Real People to help throw off the Americans.

An older man from the Ani-Yun Wiya town of Coosawatee rose to talk. The Chosen One recognized him. He had been traveling among them from town to town, farm to farm, saying now was the time to finally defeat the whites and live again in the old way. He called himself The Shadow.

Nanye'hi wanted to have nothing to do with The Shadow. But everyone had to listen to him. His message rang with just enough truth to make people want to hope he was right.

"See what has happened to us!" The Shadow yelled. "See how weak we have become! We no longer walk with our fathers. We forget how the world began. We do not remember the old stories or honor the old ways.

"We love to dress like white men, wearing their leather boots. Our women love their pots and their cloth dresses and their mirrors and beads. We sleep in beds and eat at tables. Our children read the white man's books, sing the white man's songs.

"This is why we have no game, this is why we find no deer or turkey in the forests. The natural earth has abandoned us because we have abandoned it. The spirits are ashamed of us.

"Now we must change or forever lose ourselves," The Shadow said as the people listened. "Throw away all the white man's things. Take off his clothes. Put his beds and pots and things outside your door. Take his books out of the children's hands. Dress in the skins of deer. Put on your old paint. Be the Real People again. It is the only way. It is our last chance!"

Many of the people liked what they heard. Nanye'hi, though, was saddened by it, knowing this sort of talk could only lead to more war. Then Ridge stood, speaking quietly. Ridge had fought the Americans, raided the white settlements, killed his share of people and narrowly avoided being killed many times.

"I have something to say to those who listen to The Shadow," Ridge said. "Listening to his talk will bring us war with the Americans, and that will destroy us. Yes, we have the white man's things in our lives and not all of them are good. They harm us. Yes, we all agree on that. But we must have no war against the whites, or all may die."

Just then two men who followed The Shadow ran out and attacked Ridge with their knives. Quick as ever, Ridge sidestepped them but they turned again and were upon him.

The Chosen One bolted up and pulled one of them off Ridge. Other men came up to help. But The Chosen One then was fighting this wild man, whose eyes burned with hatred for him. He wrestled as well as he could but the man's knife cut his side, sweeping down in a slashing arc. The others pulled the screaming man away before he could kill The Chosen One, pushing him back to the edge of the crowd.

The Shadow shouted loud then. "One day soon the Thunderers will bring a great storm and cover all of you with fire, all of you except the true Ani-Yun Wiya. I see it coming, and I see the truth! The true Ani-Yun Wiya will come with me to the Land of Blue Smoke and we will wait out the storm. Then we will come back and live on our land as the spirits intended us to live. So be it."

He walked away from Ustanali then, away from the council fire, away from Ridge and The Chosen One and Nanye'hi, and went to his mountain. Some people followed, selling everything they owned to be with him, to live there in the hills as the old people had done when forced to hide from their enemies.

Nanye'hi came to The Chosen One. "Let me fix that wound," she said.

"I need nothing," he said.

"Maybe, but you also might die from it," she said. So he let her treat him with a mixture of roots and clay.

Ridge spoke with him as she worked. "You are a brave man," he said.

"A foolish one," Nanye'hi said.

"That too, possibly," Ridge said. "But I want to thank you."

"It's nothing," The Chosen One said. "I liked what you said. Someone has to say what's right."

"And what is right?" Ridge asked. "I wish I knew."

Later the council voted not to fight with the young Creeks. "If there will be a fight, we fight on the side of the Americans," Ridge said, and the others voted that it would be so.

Eleven

A terrible civil war broke out among the Creeks. The ones who wanted to throw off the Americans were called the Red Sticks because they carried bright red war clubs. Beginning in the year 1813, the Red Sticks raided their own people. They burned everything that came from the whites: clothes, pots and pans, crops. They even slaughtered the beef cattle and sheep and hogs many of the Creeks kept to feed themselves.

The Red Sticks also fought United States soldiers when they came across them. On a hot summer day in south Alabama, hundreds and hundreds of Red Stick warriors attacked Fort Mims. They rushed through the gate and killed the soldiers and mixed-blood Creeks who were hiding inside. By the end of the day they had killed five hundred people, counting the mixed-bloods and whites together.

After this, the Creeks who opposed the Red Sticks asked Ridge and the Cherokees to help them. They called the Red Stick uprising the Tecumseh illness, after the Shawano leader who had traveled among their people calling for them to fight against anything white.

Ridge agreed the Cherokees must help. He and a Cherokee army of 200 men joined with General Andrew Jackson, a Tennessean and a fighting man. Jackson didn't like the Creeks, nor did he like the Cherokees much better. As he saw them, they were only in the way of white settlers.

But he accepted Ridge's offer to fight with him. He dressed Ridge's men like whites but had each of them wear two white feathers and a squirrel's tail in their hair. That way Jackson's soldiers could easily see they were not Red Sticks.

The Chosen One rode with Ridge's men. So did Five Killer, despite Nanye'hi's objections. The truth did not lie in fighting, she said. This war with the Red Sticks would come to nothing. The true war lay in educating themselves so they could fight with the whites on their own terms, with laws, as citizens of the United States.

But The Chosen One and Five Killer rode with the army, anyway. The lure of battle was still strong on the men of the Ani-Yun Wiya. The Chosen One had never ridden in battle and wanted to see how he would perform under fire. Five Killer, who had been in battle, felt he had to go even though he was no longer a young man. In fact, to a young man, Five Killer seemed old.

But they could not be persuaded to stay behind when Ridge took his men to Jackson's camp. "Maybe if the United States sees us fight for them, they will give us honor," Five Killer said. "Then perhaps we can keep our land and live in peace. That is why we fight."

But for a long time there was little fighting. Mostly, they stayed in camp with the American soldiers and did nothing. The Chosen One was restless. He had come to fight, not sit around a fire and eat corn mush all day.

Finally, in November they found the Red Sticks at Talladega, Alabama. Their enemies fought a little while, then ran away. There was shooting, shouting, screaming, lots of smoke, and then nothing. Then The Chosen One's group rode into a Red Stick town and shot down many of them. They took the women and children prisoner, along with the Red Sticks' slaves, and raided their houses, taking everything of value before burning them.

The Chosen One and Five Killer sat on their horses watching all this, saddened by what they saw. These Red Sticks, the ones they had been told were so fierce, had hardly put up a fight. Their women and children were much like those of the Ani-Yun Wiya back home. They were not so different from the people The Chosen One and Five Killer had known all their lives.

Maybe Nanye'hi had been right. Maybe nothing was being proven here on the battlefield.

Soon after that fight, winter was upon the army. Jackson's own men, bored and muddy and hungry, began to drift off to their farms and towns. When the men of the Ani-Yun Wiya went home, they drove before them the horses and cattle they had captured from the Red Sticks towns.

Andrew Jackson, angry that his men left before the war was over, called for them to return to camp. So after the winter ended, Ridge returned with 500 more men mounted on fine horses, some taken from the Red Sticks the previous fall.

"Don't go," Nanye'hi told The Chosen One and Five Killer.

"Please stay home," The Fawn begged.

Still, they had to go. Something about Jackson drew them in. Something about Ridge made it impossible to say no.

By the time the weather warmed in 1814, they were there in camp again, eating corn mush, watching soldiers drill. Ridge was now called Major Ridge, promoted by Jackson himself, and he proudly wore his new rank, sitting even taller on his horse than before.

This is not something a man can miss, The Chosen One told himself.

When the army finally marched after the Red Sticks, Ridge's men rode in front, watching for the enemy. Along the way, friendly Creeks joined them. There was almost no fighting at all, and everything seemed simple, a few thousand men wandering through the Alabama wilderness doing nothing much.

Then near the end of March, following the Tallapoosa River, the scouts found Red Sticks camped ahead. They were at a big bend in the river, with a thousand heavily-armed warriors and their women supplying them as they hid behind a protective breastworks of logs.

For a while, Jackson's men and the Cherokees stayed on their side of the river wondering how to cross it without getting shot by the Red Sticks. The Chosen One, standing with Ridge, had noticed some Creek canoes on the oposite side of the river.

"If we had those canoes, we could cross several groups at a time," he said.

"Yes, but getting them would be no easy thing," Ridge said.

"I can do it," The Chosen One said.

"Maybe we should wait until something happens, then go," Ridge said.

"And we will wait all day and night. We have to cross now," he said.

With that, he went to the water's edge and dove in. Two other men saw him and followed. Ridge's men began shooting at the Red Sticks as the three began to swim the river. As they got closer, bullets began kicking up the water around them, so they swam underwater, surfacing only to breathe.

When they came to the canoes, one of the other men was shot. Even so, he kept moving, helping The Chosen One untie the canoes. He was too badly hurt to take the canoes to the other side, though, and stayed behind as The Chosen One and the other man made it across the river with several canoes.

The canoes helped the first men cross the river. Once they landed on the Red Sticks' side of the river, the battle truly started. By this time, some more of Jackson's men were on the other side of the bend, shooting at the Red Sticks so they were caught in a crossfire.

Bullets hit all around The Chosen One. Five Killer rushed up to him. "That was crazy, swimming after those canoes," he said, as they hid behind a big rock.

"It worked, didn't it?" The Chosen One said.

"What if it had failed?"

"I do not think about failure."

Five Killer grunted and laughed. He looked around toward the Red Sticks behind their wall of logs. Just then a bullet chipped the rock a foot from his face so he jumped back down.

"Now who's crazy?" The Chosen One said.

Finally, Jackson's army rushed the Red Sticks, fighting hand-to-hand. The Chosen One ran forward with the others, losing sight of Five Killer. He hit one Red Stick man in the head with his rifle, then ducked another as he jumped him from the log breastworks. He pulled out his knife and stabbed the man as they rolled over, stabbing him again and again until he lay still. Then a woman charged him from behind with a red war club.

He heard her running at him and looked up in time to dodge her. But she picked up a knife from the ground and ran at him again. As she swiped at him, the edge of the blade cut his forehead so blood ran down into his eyes.

Wiping it away, he saw the woman was fairly young, looking a lot like The Fawn. She was trim and light on her feet. Her hair was long and falling free across her shoulders. But her eyes were filled with hatred.

He didn't want to kill her. He wondered what he should do if she charged him again, flailing at him with that knife. She took two steps toward him, then fell, killed by a bullet through the heart.

He looked around for his savior but saw no one. Perhaps the man with the gun had already gone on.

Few of the Red Sticks ran. Those who did jumped in the water and swam away. The Chosen One saw the Red Stick leader, Weatherford, a mixed-blood Creek, on a beautiful dark horse dive from a cliff into the water, getting away before the army could reach him.

And then the battle was over. Nothing was left but its aftermath, and that was very ugly.

The Chosen One was sickened by what he saw. He stumbled over to Five Killer, who also stood and watched the army celebrate the victory, disgust on his face.

They saw Andrew Jackson walk across the battlefield, his officers following. He stopped at a pile of bodies of Red Stick women, reaching down for something. It was a baby that he pulled out. He lifted the child high, laughing as they watched, then brought it down and kissed its cheek.

Handing it to one of his officers to keep for him, he said he would take it home. He would raise it himself. The general stood there looking at his prize like a child might look upon a new puppy.

The Chosen One and Five Killer looked upon this with a sort of wonder. How could Jackson kill the child's family, then turn around and kiss its cheek and adopt it? Would the Creek child just be another toy for the general, something on the order of a race-horse or a new pair of boots? The Chosen One wondered what sort of life this child would live, what sort of love he would find.

Whatever happened to him, it wouldn't be easy growing up in Jackson's house.

The Chosen One

This Jackson, this general and Tennessean, this white man who led them to the river of death, was indeed a strange one.

Twelve

He should have listened to Nanye'hi, the Chosen One thought. He should never have gone to this river of death in Alabama. Hundreds and hundreds of the Creeks died before the guns of Jackson's men. Some white soldiers died, too, and 18 of the Real People. It was a terrible thing.

For many days after the battle, he could not forget what happened there. Jackson called it The Battle of Horseshoe Bend. It seemed more like slaughter than a battle to the Chosen One, though. From now on, he knew, the Creeks would never be the same. There would be nothing to stop settlement in their country. The Real People would live on an island of land surrounded by white Americans.

The Chosen One turned homeward with the other warriors. They spoke quietly among themselves riding to the Georgia villages, the home of Ridge and other leaders. If Jackson's guns could do that to the Creeks, they could also do it to the Real People, they said. We must counsel, they said. We must think.

The white soldiers from east Tennessee had beaten them to the Georgia farms and villages, stealing horses, killing hogs and cows, wrecking gardens, taking anything they found. Some of the warriors wanted to ride after them to take back their property. But Ridge stopped them.

"Enough of fighting!" he said. "Enough of killing! Let us learn to live in peace together. We have seen what comes of fighting."

So they settled down to their farms, and the Chosen One rode on to the Ocoee and his family. He held The Fawn in his arms and decided to never leave her again. He would not take up the gun or the knife. Enough war, he said. Let there be no more war. He would live in peace.

Visiting Nanye'hi, he was shocked to find her looking so old. She moved slowly, like an old woman, but still talked with all the power of the young woman he had known as a child.

"I hear of bad things in the Creek country," she said.

"Don't make me tell it," he said.

"There is no need to speak of it," she said. "I know. The wind carries the sadness. The Creeks were our enemies in the long ago but nothing good comes of war like this. In times such as these, all peoples should come together in strength."

She moved to the hearth, checking the bread baking there. He watched closely. Her fingers, old as she was, were still strong, clean, certain of their work. Her face seemed to glow in the dim light, the skin still lovely.

"What does the wind tell you about the Real People?" he asked.

"Why must you know this?" she asked.

"I want to understand it."

"There is no understanding for such things," she said. "And it is not the wind that tells me, but my heart. I feel bad things coming, and much sadness. I think we must leave this place, and it is holy to us. In any other place, we will be a different people because the people are a part of the earth where they are born. Take us from this place and I fear bad things will happen to us."

"But you say we should not fight," he said.

She took the bread from the hearth, setting it on the table to cool. "All my life I have seen fighting," she said. "I became the Beloved Woman in a fight with the Creeks, never forget that. But I have seen nothing good come from all this fighting. I have seen many terrible things and much death in these wars. But no one wins. We all lose when we fight."

"But how can we stay here without a fight?" he asked.

She looked at him, then beyond him as though she was looking into the darkest days of the future. "For some things there is no answer," she said. "And I will be of no help to you or anyone when this happens."

"Why not?"

"Why, I'll be dead, of course," she said. "I am an old woman. Surely you don't expect me to live forever."

He cut a piece of bread and began to eat, watching her sit silently across the table. Then he realized that he had expected her to be with them always. A world without Nanye'hi would be a dark world indeed.

Thirteen

Though Strong Girl, now grown up and called Strong Woman by nearly everyone, was no blood relation, The Chosen One thought of her as his sister. That made her son, Black Fox, his nephew, and men of the Real People helped their nephews as they journeyed to manhood.

As the boy grew, he took him on hunts, showing him the secrets of the bow and arrow and spear even though Black Fox was more interested in the rifle, which outdated the old ways. He showed the boy proper methods to set traps and to skin out the animals caught in them.

More often, though, they spent time riding to speak to other men of the Real People. The people were worried and angry. More and more these days the whites talked of sending them west to a wild country that would be dangerous and far from home.

A few of the Real People had already gone there, giving up their land at home. From some who drifted back homeward, the people heard terrible things of this western country. There were hostile tribes already living there who thought of them as invaders. They fought fiercely, making anything the Creeks of old did seem like child's play.

Most of the people wanted to stay right where they had always been, far from the violence of the west. Some men, though, thought going west would allow them to run free as they had in the past, far away from the whites and those who tried to tell them how to live. They could hunt as a man was supposed to do, leaving all this farming for the women.

In the west, they said, wild game was plentiful. The country was wide open. A man could live out his life like a real man, not as a farmer scratching the thin soils of Georgia and Tennessee.

This kind of talk worried The Chosen One. He wanted to stay here at home in the country of his birth. The Beloved Woman always said they should keep their land. Make no more paper talks, she said, make no more treaties.

He believed that was the only way for the Real People. What would they be in another country? This country in the shadows of the Land of Blue Smoke was theirs and they belonged to it. They could not leave.

Riding the roads with Black Fox, he explained these things to the boy.

"But don't you think it would be exciting to go out west?" the boy asked.

"For a day or a week or even a month, but not to live," he said. "That is not our place in the world. This land we live upon is sacred to us."

He took Black Fox back to the old places, to see the greatness of his people. They first rode to Chota, the town along the river where Nanye'hi had taken him in as a lost and lonely child. There, the whites were everywhere. Seeing them ride alongside a corn field, a man came running from a log home, cursing them.

"Dirty Indians!" he yelled at them, then raised a rifle and fired a shot at them.

The Chosen One reined in his nervous horse, sitting straight and looking at the white man. Black Fox sat just as straight beside him. The white man trembled as he tried to get off another shot.

"You have nothing to fear from us," The Chosen One told him.

"What do you want?" the white man asked.

"You are living on my land. Your crops grow in my soil," he said.

"I got a deed," the white man said. "This is mine and you better get off it."

"A deed is just paper. It means nothing," The Chosen One said, and rode away in seilence followed by Black Fox.

He walked the horse along the edge of the river, finding the old path where he'd walked so many times before. He showed the boy the little pile of stones where Nanye'hi added a stone each time she passed by, in memory of one who died long ago.

For her, he found a small stone and added it to the pile. Black Fox did this, also. They stood silently as a crow flew overhead screaming out its cawing cry.

Then they rode upstream, toward the place where The Chosen One was born. They found only the ruins of that old village. Briars and weeds covered everything.

The Chosen One told Black Fox his memories of the sickness that spread among so many of the people there, of how they died in such great numbers there had been fear of burying them properly. He explained how he had left there, sent by his dying mother to search for the Beloved Woman.

"What was your mother's name?" Black Fox asked. "Tell me about her."

"I do not remember," he said. "I think of her as being like the wind, something great that covers all things, yet something I can never see or touch."

He sat on the horse, looking at the place where his people had lived, and the trees shimmering overhead and the river flowing gently nearby. There was nothing here for him, yet somehow everything that counted was here. This was where he'd started his journey. This was a spot forever holy.

Fourteen

One night The Chosen One dreamed about a journey to the sunrise. He and his cousins the wolves were walking in the darkness together, led by a great white swan. He was very tired but the swan was strong and swift and led them to a place where the sky touched the ground. He saw a hole in the ground, with the sun far away and coming toward him.

The swan sat with him a while, then walked to the hole in the ground. "It is my time to go," the swan told him.

His cousins the wolves gathered around and told the swan to stay. "We will be lost without you," they said.

"You have noses to smell the way home, and good heads to know what to do," the swan told them. "I must go on without you."

So the swan flapped her wings and flew into the hole, soaring toward the sun. The Chosen One watched her until the light hurt his eyes and he had to look away.

When he woke up, he knew what the dream meant. He went outside, saddled his horse, and rode quickly away to the Beloved Woman's house. Once there he found Strong Woman and Black Fox, Five Killer, and many of Nanye'hi's grandchildren.

He took Five Killer aside. Five Killer said, "There is nothing to be done. Even the Beloved Woman must die sometime."

They spent that day sitting with her, watching her breathe as she lay in her bed, holding her hands, speaking quietly. When she died, some said they saw a white swan leave her body and fly away toward Chota. But The Chosen One wasn't sure what he saw. He only knew she was gone forever and life would now be different.

Five Killer looked old. The Chosen One himself felt tired and knew he had gray in his hair. He stood beside Strong Woman, the only sister he'd known, and began to cry, not just for the Beloved

Woman, but for them all, for the hard times and the good times past and the times to come which they must now face without the Beloved Woman. Strong Woman, a widow now herself, reached up and wiped the tears from his face with her fingers, then pulled his head to hers and they held each other, saying nothing.

When he rode home, pushing the horse hard, he felt alone, that all of his people were now alone. At his house, he sat by himself under a poplar tree for many hours, trying to think of what must be done. But nothing came to him. He felt empty.

For a long time afterward, he was filled with emptiness. Finally, he went to Georgia to visit with Ridge. They went to the council meeting at the new capital of their people, New Echota, where all the talk was about whether they would move west to Indian Territory, leaving their native country to the whites.

He remembered the old capital, Chota, his childhood home, and saw nothing like it in this new one. There were only two houses here. Two houses! Some capital town this was. An open-sided council house was there for the meetings, and a log house for the clerks who kept track of the people's business.

Ridge, calling himself Major Ridge after his title during the Creek War with Jackson, was everywhere at this meeting, riding a big strong horse. He welcomed the white commissioners, laughed with the representatives of their old enemies, the Creeks, and discussed with everyone the question of whether the Real People should move.

The Chosen One watched all this, thinking about the Beloved Woman's words against giving up their land. He spoke to Ridge about this. Ridge replied, "We will stay right here, where our fathers spilled their blood. This is our country and we will not let anyone take it."

The Ridge talked about the new written language of their people invented by Sequoya. They would have a newspaper in their own language, and books. They would model their political system on the United States, building a Supreme Court, and a Congress. They would have schools and libraries and towns just like the whites.

Times must change. The Chosen One understood this. But he knew that the Real People would not survive by copying the whites. He went home, tended his chickens, hunted when he could, worked with his family in the fields, and worried about all the changes coming for his people.

He watched the children of the Real People grow up knowing more about the white society than their own. He tried to teach them all the things he had learned from the Beloved Woman but they were not very interested in the old ways or the old stories of the Real People. They wanted to move ahead, to become part of something new.

Impossible. He told himself that we are what we were just as we are what we become. Deny that and everything loses its meaning.

Over the years, the Real People signed more treaties giving away land. At New Echota, they built their Supreme Court building and their newspaper, edited by an educated young man named Elias Boudinot, who wrote against giving up any more of their land.

But one day word came to The Chosen One that disturbed him very much. Andrew Jackson had been elected president of the United States. He remembered Jackson at the Battle of Horseshoe Bend, giving orders to slaughter the Creeks, then getting off his horse to save that Creek child on the battlefield. Jackson was not a man to trust, he thought.

Something very bad would come of this. He recalled Jackson's face, all those years ago, with its look of hatred even for the Real People who fought beside him.

Jackson elected president! It was a sad day, The Chosen One thought. He felt as though he was riding a running horse just ahead of a swift violent storm that would soon overtake him.

Fifteen

The trouble started in Georgia, when gold was discovered on the lands of the Real People. The state government there passed laws taking away their property. According to the law, they had no more rights than a mule or a dog. Their Supreme Court, their Congress, their laws meant nothing to the whites.

The Chosen One rode to Georgia to see for himself what was happening to the Real People. The state gave lottery tickets to each white citizen, and they drew lots to see which piece of Cherokee land was theirs. Some white men armed themselves and rode from farm to farm, shooting and harassing the people, burning houses and barns.

All for a rock, The Chosen One thought, for gold so that women may wear fancy jewelry.

Still the Cherokees refused to leave their country. The whites drew up treaty after treaty that would force them to go. But most of them were too proud to run from a bunch of gold-crazed land thieves.

Even when John Ross, the new leader of the Real People, was arrested, they would not go. The whites stopped them from publishing their newspaper, *The Cherokee Phoenix*, and shut down their schools. Then they gathered 300 men, women and children at New Echota and had them sign a treaty selling all their land for five million dollars. They agreed to move to Indian Territory in the west.

No man of importance signed that paper. John Ross and their leaders sent a letter to Washington saying the treaty was not official, with the signatures of 16,000 Cherokees. The Chosen One was proud to put his name on Ross's letter. But it all came to nothing. Congress gave them two years to leave their homeland and move to the wilderness.

Some of the young men now wanted to fight the whites. Years ago, when he was young, The Chosen One would have, too. But now he saw it was hopeless. If they fought, they would lose everything. Still, many of the Real People armed themselves and moved into the mountains, living on roots and small animals, waiting for the battle to come.

The United States sent an army of 7,000 men to the Cherokee country to make sure they moved without a fight. It was hopeless and the people began to come in from the hills, laying down their weapons.

The Chosen One watched all this with sadness. Andrew Jackson was no longer president of the United States. A man named Martin Van Buren took his place but continued to push the Cherokees from their land. It was Jackson who started this, he thought. Jackson could have stopped it if he wanted.

Jackson, the old Indian fighter, turned against his friends the Cherokees and betrayed them. Without them, Jackson would never have won at Horseshoe Bend. He would never have become president of the United States. Now he spit on them and ran them from their homes.

The Chosen One remembered that battle at Horseshoe Bend and how easily he could have killed Jackson. If he had done it, he would certainly have been killed himself. But his people might have been spared this pain.

There was no way of knowing, all those years ago, what would happen in the years to come. But if The Chosen One had known, he would have turned his rifle on Jackson and spilled the betrayer's blood on the battlefield. Perhaps they would still have been run off their land, but Jackson would not have been the one that did it.

One day The Chosen One was working in his corn field when white soldiers appeared. They carried rifles with bayonets. The one in charge stepped forward and said, "It's time you were going. Get your things."

He stood watching the soldiers, considering what to do. He was old and they were young. He had no chance against them. So he went to the house with them. More soldiers were there, waiting with The Fawn.

He held her close. She softly cried until the soldiers forced them apart.

"Get moving," one of the soldiers said. "Lazy, shiftless Indians, that's what you all are."

"You are thieves," The Fawn said. "You take what is not yours. You want something for nothing. We worked hard for all this. You did nothing for it. Now you take it but it will never belong to you. It is ours for all time."

"Quit your yapping," the soldier said. "You've got ten minutes to clear out."

So they gathered what they could, mounted two horses, and rode with the soldiers to a huge make-shift camp of the Real People. They were forced to leave behind their cows and other horses, their dogs, everything they could not easily carry.

In the camp, they saw people crying, people sitting on the ground staring at nothing, people who had lost everything and had little reason to continue living. He searched through the camp until he found his daughter, Swan, and her husband, a man named John Hart, though he was one of the Real People. They had their own son now, an eight-year-old named Jimmy.

He took Jimmy with him looking through the camp, and found Strong Woman, with her son Black Fox and his wife, named Robin, or Tsiskwa'gwa in their own language. They had a six-year-old daughter named Susannah.

Strong Woman came to him and took his hand, tears in her eyes. "We are going to the ghost country," she said.

He said nothing. Their people always called the west, 'the ghost country'. They meant, 'land of the dead'. It was somewhere toward where the sun set. They had never been there, but now they were on their way.

Susannah ran to him and he held her close in one arm, with his other hand on Strong Woman's shoulder. There was nothing to say, nothing to do.

He and The Fawn moved in with their kinfolk and friends. Now they could only wait.

Sixteen

It was September, still hot as mid-summer, when the troops rousted them from camp and set them on the long road westward. The older people were weak and fearful, the young men wild and in a rage at being imprisoned for nothing. Through the long summer they had been packed tightly together, sick and full of fever.

Each family had a wagon to carry its belongings and supplies, pulled by oxen or horses or sometimes mules. The Chosen One's group included Swan and her family, and Strong Woman with Black Fox and his family. The wagon was crowded. They let the children ride as the men walked alongside driving the horses.

Looking back at the procession, they could see hundreds of others winding along the muddy road. Crossing the Tennessee River at Blythe's Ferry along the Hiwassee River, they felt at home. But as they turned westward toward McMinnville and on toward Nashville, they entered a new and foreign country where most of them had never journeyed before.

The Chosen One remembered this country from the hunting trips of his youth. It was good land but nothing like home, and nothing like where they were going, he supposed.

Walking day after day weakened them all. He saw The Fawn grow more and more tired until one day she could not rise to eat breakfast.

"You'll go on today without me," she said, lying on the ground next to the wagon.

"Never," he said. "I'll never go without you."

He sat beside her, not moving, holding her hand, until he realized at last she was dead.

A soldier rode by on his horse and tossed The Chosen One a shovel. "Hurry up," he said. "There's no time to waste on crying."

Together, they dug a grave and lowered The Fawn into it. They stood over her body in silence, then covered her with earth until at last she was gone.

Two days later, Black Fox swung an axe handle at a Georgia soldier who pushed him from behind, hurrying him along. The soldier pointed a rifle at Black Fox and smiled as he shot him down. They buried him that night after the wagons stopped for supper.

Strong Woman's grief was so great that The Chosen One realized she would be the next to die. "I have no reason to live," she said.

"You have a granddaughter," he said.

"But I have no country," she said. "Why should I go on?"

Three days later, before they reached Nashville, sick with fever and stomach pains, she died.

The march became an agony for everyone. They moved out as day broke, then walked as far as they could. Wagon wheels broke and had to be fixed. Sick people fell to the side and required care. Those who died had to be buried.

It was a hard time, very hard. His grandson Jimmy caught the measles and died. After burying him, Swan and her husband disappeared one night. He never saw them again. That left The Chosen One, Black Fox's wife Robin, and her daughter, Susannah.

Walking alongside the wagon as Susannah rode, Robin sang. Her voice was lovely, even if she didn't remember the old songs. She made them up as she went along. He enjoyed hearing her. But there was a sadness about her, something that carried all the agony of this march in her body.

She tended the sick as they went along. Then one day in western Kentucky, she herself fell in the wagon track. As he buried her, The Chosen One felt very weak. He knew he was sick, too. If he died, Susannah would have no one left in this world to care for her.

But even with that thought in mind, he felt himself sinking down, flush with fever, a sharp pain in his lungs. He coughed blood and had trouble breathing.

Some white settlers from nearby came to see the Cherokees on their march. A man and woman stood over The Chosen One as he lay there, struggling to live.

"Don't touch him," the man said. "He's full of diseases."

The woman looked at Susannah standing nearby. "We could use that girl," she said. "I need some help in the kitchen and she could be put to work in the fields."

"It's another mouth to feed," the man said.

"We'll make her work for her keep," the woman said.

They led Susannah away into the night. The girl looked back at The Chosen One, calling for help.

He tried to go after her, but his legs would not work. His lungs screamed for air. He could do nothing. So he lay there, thinking about the lost Susannah and all the other lost ones, and he cried.

At sunrise, he was still alive. Someone loaded him onto a wagon with some other sick ones, and a shaman hovered over him, chanting something he couldn't understand. The shaman sprinkled water on his face, then smoked a pipe and blew tobacco smoke into his mouth. The Chosen One heard him mumbling, telling the witches to keep away from this man.

They came to another river, and he was still alive. The shaman took him from the wagon and bathed him in the freezing water. A white doctor came to look at him and did nothing but shake his head.

A night passed, then another, and another. He decided that since he had made it this long, he would probably live. After another day, he got up from the wagon and began to walk, so that other sick ones might have room to ride.

After many days they reached Indian Territory. He stood on the foreign ground and thought about the graves, so many shallow graves following their trail all along the way. His family, every one, was gone.

Only he, an old man survived. He shouldn't be here. It should be Jimmy or Swan or Black Fox. Life wasn't fair. He had always known this but now he had proof in his own living, breathing body.

Seventeen

In the Territory, he wound up spending much of his time with Ridge at a place known as Honey Creek. It was not bad land, but not so good as what they had at home.

Ridge was an old man now, too. He and his group had traveled on a steamboat more than a year before The Chosen One's family left on their doomed trip west. Ridge had come by water and even part of the way on railroad cars. None of his family was lost on the journey.

Ridge was busy making a plantation of his new land, using money he had been paid for improvements to his land in Georgia. One day The Chosen One asked Ridge what he heard of Yonaguska and the people who escaped high into the mountains of the Land of Blue Smoke, staying behind when all the others were forced westward.

"I hear nothing of them, and I think nothing of them. We are different people now," Ridge said.

But The Chosen One didn't feel different. Riding across Indian Territory, he knew he would always be a stranger in this new country. There was a good deal of arguing among the people, too. Those who had come years earlier wanted to keep their own form of government. The recent arrivals had agreed to maintain the laws they had at home.

Worst of all, John Ross's group of men accused Ridge's people of selling their Georgia land to the whites. This was forbidden by Cherokee law, and now Ross's men were ready to punish them for it. In three separate attacks, they killed Ridge's son, John, the newspaperman Elias Boudinot, and Ridge himself.

All this sickened The Chosen One. He wanted nothing to do with politics, nothing to do with murder, especially of any of the Real People. If the Beloved Woman could have known about this, she would have been very sad. He knew she loved her people, all of her people. Any fight like this was wrong and she would have stood against it.

But The Chosen One wanted to go home. He was old and had no strength to make a stand against any fight. So the night after Ridge's murder, he saddled his horse and slowly rode eastward, setting out toward the place where the sun rises from the hole in the ground.

That first night, he slept on the ground and dreamed about a swan leading the way toward the Land of Blue Smoke. In the dream, he saw himself and also a small girl, both going home, to Yonaguska's band hiding in the mountains.

Next day, he pushed the horse harder, knowing where he rode. He passed the shallow graves along the way where they had buried their people on the removal to Indian Territory. Many of the graves had been disturbed, dug up by people looking for the jewelry and other things of value that might have been buried with the dead.

He crossed the Mississippi River on a ferry, then set off through western Kentucky. When they passed this way before, he had been so sick that it was hard to remember exactly where they had been. But he followed the trail of graves and discarded belongings until he came to the right place.

This was the spot where Robin died. He searched until finding her grave, pausing there to think about her sacrifice. On the horse again, he began to look for the houses of white settlers. After deciding two cabins were not what he was looking for, he came to the right one.

He saw the child Susannah, pulling weeds in a corn field, watched over by a large bearded white man. The man was gruff and yelled at her often in a loud, coarse voice.

The Chosen One dismounted and hid his horse well back in the woods nearby. At the edge of the clearing, he watched the girl. After working in the field, the man and Susanna stopped to eat lunch under a tree at the house. The man tossed her some meat as he might a dog and she ate it with her fingers. He drank from a jug, then let her have whatever was left. A white boy and girl began to eat and drink, laughing with their father, and the boy began tossing small stones at Susannah.

A woman came out and talked with the man. After eating, he left Susannah with the woman, who put her to work washing clothes in a big tub of water sitting on a fire. The Chosen One thought she was working hard for a young child but the woman picked up a stick and hit her across the back when she stopped to rest.

The woman went inside the house, leaving Susannah outside working while the other two children played nearby. The Chosen One got his horse, tightened the cinch and mounted, easing to the edge of the clearing.

He paused there, seeing the man busy again in the corn field. The woman was still inside. So he kicked the horse and it began to run full-speed through the clearing.

The boy looked up and saw him first. "Injuns!" he yelled. "Red devils!"

But The Chosen One paid him no mind. Susannah looked up and started to run toward the house with the other children. But the horse was racing as fast as it could now and he cut her off before she could reach the cabin. The woman had come just outside the door and was screaming for the man to bring his gun. But The Chosen One leaned over as the horse ran, reached out, and pulled Susannah onto the saddle with him. The horse never slowed as it ran from the clearing and through the woods.

Susannah was crying but he could do nothing about that. He kept the horse off the road, running through the valleys and creeks, always heading east. After a long time, when he was sure it was safe, he slowed the horse to a trot, then a walk. Finally, they stopped, and he put Susannah on the ground, jumping down beside her.

She was small and thin, no bigger than she had been when those people took her as he lay sick on the ground.

"Where are we going?" she asked.

"Home," he said. "We are going home. I came to take you home."

"Away from those people," she said. "I know you. I remember a lot of people sick and dying, and you were there. Your name is The Chosen One."

"Yes, and your name is Susannah."

"I remember," she said. "Those people, they just called me any old thing they wanted. They weren't nice."

"I know, but that's all over," he said.

"Are you my grandfather?" she asked.

"Not really, but I can be if you want me to be."

"I do," she said. "I need somebody that I belong to."

"So do I," he said. "So do I."

"Grandfather, why do they call you The Chosen One?" she asked. "That's a strange name."

He pulled the child close. She sat on the ground next to him. Looking into the depths of those perfect dark eyes, he saw the life of the Real People, all the things of the past and all the things to come.

He touched her face, smiled, and said, "I want to tell you about a faraway sacred place known as Chota a long, long time ago and a little lost boy who by the greatest of miracles was saved by a person we called the Beloved Woman."

And so he told his story. He had never told it before, but now it was time. Susannah listened quietly until he finished. Then they mounted the horse and rode toward home.

Afterword

The Ani-Yun Wiya called themselves the Real People. American settlers moving into their region called them Cherokees, though the origin of that name remains a mystery.

Nanye'hi, the Beloved Woman of the Cherokees, was also known as Nancy Ward. She was probably born in the late 1730s, before her people were greatly infuenced by European settlers. By the time she died, in 1822, their way of life had been changed forever by the swirl of events around them.

The Beloved Woman did give a home to her people's children orphaned by disease and war. Children like The Chosen One and Strong Girl owed their lives to her. Though their real stories are lost in the history of the Real People, we can be sure they were no less dramatic than that of The Chosen One.

About the Author

Charles Blake Johnson wrote *The Last Beloved Woman*, a fictional biography about Nanye'hi, or Nancy Ward, the Beloved Woman of the Cherokees. He is also Southern editor of *Farm Journal* magazine. His other books include *Bailout*, an adventure novel. With his wife Patti and daughter Ellen, he lives in the Smoky Mountains of Tennessee, which the Real People call The Land of Blue Smoke.